FREEDOM, 250,000 BC

OUT FROM THE SHADOW OF POPOCATÉPETL

BONNYE MATTHEWS

Award Winning Writer
of Prehistoric Fiction

PO Box 221974 Anchorage, Alaska 99522-1974
books@publicationconsultants.com—www.publicationconsultants.com

ISBN 978-1-59433-633-1
eBook ISBN Number: 978-1-59433-669-0

Library of Congress Catalog Card Number: 2016954277

Copyright 2016 Bonnye Matthews
—First Edition—

Cover Image of Mountain: Tlazotlalizti CCA-SA 4

Manufactured in the United States of America.

Acknowledgments

Without the assistance of several people *Freedom, 250,000 BC* would not be. These people are my brother, Randy Matthews, and then Sally Sutherland, Patricia Gilmore, Robert Arthur, Pat Meiwes, and Rebecca Goodrich. Each contributed far in excess of what could be expected or hoped for based on family, friendship, or love of reading. I also thank my publisher, Evan Swensen, who had the courage to take on this project.

Award Winning Winds of Change Book Series

Exordium

I received an invitation from the storyteller, Muz. At the campfire I sit, prepared to listen to his new Place History. His voice is deep, resonant, each word pronounced carefully and completely. He holds my attention magnetically, so I never wander from the story. Time stops for me. Tiny little cinders fly skywards above the campfire in a timeless world. Tonight Muz tells the story of a young man, Wing. Occasionally he looks off to the side, as if he relives a bit of the story.

Muz is bent over, an exceedingly wrinkled old man, bow-legged from old age. He wears a simple animal skin skirt, as worn as is he. The skirt dangles raggedly to his knees and sports a partial deboned tail on the side. He carries the scent of old dust sometimes, roses or the scent of evergreens at other times. His snarl-free, waist-length hair is white and flows freely in the breeze. He sees through its wisps with black eyes riveting forward as if nothing could possibly impede his vision at this moment or any other. His black obsidian eyes peer out from tired lids and miss nothing.

I watch the images he creates between his gnarled outstretched hands, the backs of which show huge blue veins snaking across his thin skin. Muz shows the living earth at Mexico. Traveling through time he shows me two tectonic plates: a huge North American Plate and under the curved part of Mexico out in the Pacific Ocean, the relatively tiny Cocos Plate. Pressure forms from the subduction of the Cocos Plate as it dives north under the North American Plate. Twenty million years ago when subduction began, that pressure began to cause a string of volcanoes to form in the lower part of Mexico to release magma to balance the pressure. The resulting volcanoes align from west to east across the entire country, forming the Sierra Nevada Range. Popocatépetl and La Malinque, mountains in the story, are part of this range. The Mexican Sierra Nevada is not the same as the Sierra Nevada in the United States. Sierra Nevada means snow-covered mountain range. The specific Place History Muz imparts is an area named Valsequillo, just south of the mountains. Muz tells the story so that I feel as if I'm there as it occurs.

The campfire is white crusted ashes. Time resumes for me. Muz smiles. Tired after his night of storytelling, he stands. He walks past me and stops, momentarily placing his hand on my head, sealing the story to my memory. Then, Muz walks into a golden mist and disappears, taking the mist with him. The story remains behind waiting to be written. I've known it from the past in the present. Now is the time for the present story to be prepared for the future to know.

Dedication

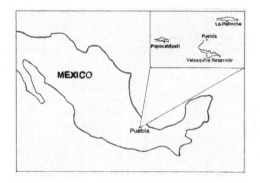

Archaeological Site at Valsequillo

Freedom, 250,000 BC is dedicated to the archaeological site south of Puebla, Mexico at the Valsequillo Reservoir. What the site shows is an amazingly rich prehistoric view of human life in the Americas, specifically Mexico, in 250,000 BC. That date is the glory and infamy of the Valsequillo site.

Two mountains are involved in this story. The title, *Freedom, 250,000 BC: Out From the Shadow of Popocatépetl,* refers to the volcanic mountain, Popocatépetl, to the northwest of the Valsequillo site. Popocatépetl is pronounced po-po-ca-te-petal, the last part like flower petal. The other mountain, La Malinche, erupted and its ash preserved the amazing finds at the site.

Introduction

There is no longer an archaeological site south of Puebla, Mexico at Valsequillo. It's been buried and hidden. Why? The answer is as old as man. It's a power war over dogmatic belief. I chose this site for the first novella in the series because of the controversy—not despite it.

In 1959 Juan Armenta Comacho, an accountant in Mexico who was fascinated by prehistoric finds in the Valsequillo area, chanced to discover a mammoth pelvis bone. He pried it from the soil. It was not an unusual find, until, when cleaning it later, he found animal carvings on the mammoth bone.

Surprisingly one of the animals was an extinct gomphothere *(Ryncotherium),* a four-tusked elephant-like animal; another, a speared feline. There were others. The find immediately generated great interest. The Smithsonian Institution featured it, and *LIFE Magazine* did a brief article showing the carving (Illustration 1). The bone had been carved when green.

In other words, it was carved when the bone was fresh. What's remarkable, and unknown at the time of the article, is that the bone scientifically dated to 250,000 years ago. That simple scientific test would set off an explosive archaeological battle over the past that continues today. There was a carver 250,000 years ago in the Americas! That was heresy in the world of evolutionary *belief*, totally plausible *scientifically*.

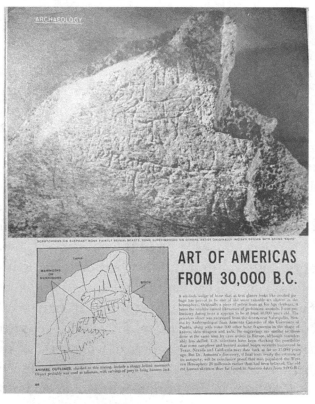

Illustration 1: *LIFE Magazine,* Volume 49, No. 7, page 86 (8/15/1960).

In addition to the engraved mammoth pelvis bone two skulls have been found that relate to man in the Americas at a very early time. Skull 1: Associated with the Valsequillo site, the Dorenberg skull, found at the Valsequillo site in the late 1800s ended up in a museum in Leipzig, Germany, where it was destroyed by bombing during WWII. It's gone.

Inside that skull there was encrustation from diatoms. Diatoms are minute photosynthesizing algae with silica cell walls, intricate in form. Hugo Reichelt in Leipzig scraped diatoms from the skull to get a sense of its date. The date of the diatoms scraping was established as "antediluvian," not a very helpful term. Essentially, it meant before the Biblical flood. Some of the diatoms were extinct 80,000 years ago.

A few decades ago, Sam L. VanLandingham, a diatom paleontologist, dated a reference slide of diatoms at the California Academy of Sciences in San Francisco. The diatoms on the slide came from the Dorenberg skull scraping. He dated the skull diatoms from between 80,000 to 220,000 years ago. Sam VanLandingham also dated diatoms at the site where the skull and artifacts had been found. The diatoms at the site dated to between 80,000 to 220,000 years before the present. The same forms of diatoms found in the soil at the site at Valsequillo and the skull scrapings are consistent in species and age.

13

Skull 2: The Ostrander skull was found in California. With the brow ridges, it's either *Homo erectus* or *Homo neanderthalensis*. Very ancient people were in the southwest part of what's now the USA and Mexico a long, long time ago. Neither skull remains available today. The first was destroyed in WWII and the second may have been given a Native American burial.

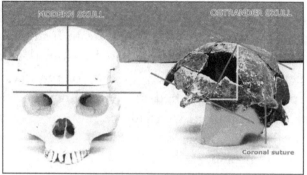

Illustration 2: Ostrander skull (on right).
Used with permission from Austin Whittall.

So what happened at Valsequillo? The wonderful bone art found by Comacho, spotlighted by the Smithsonian, and photographed in *LIFE Magazine* was dated. C-14 wouldn't go back far enough. Testing was performed using the Uranium series. The date? 250,000 years ago. Then things went haywire. The lead scientist on the site, Cynthia Irwin-Williams, refused to accept the date. Rather than face ridicule, which she knew would follow, she essentially dropped the project. Ridicule came anyway. Other problems arose. Finds were removed from the scientists and hidden or destroyed. Scientists were accused of planting finds to discredit the work. How it never occurred to anyone that no self-respecting scientist would knowingly plant finds that would cause himself to be ridiculed, I don't know.

What has been buried at the Valsequillo site is precious. Skulls, engravings, tools all once showed a site at 250,000 years ago just south of Puebla, Mexico. It's part of a potentially rich and amazing heritage in this land of ours. Nonsense brought it to the current conclusion. Maybe in time there will be an environment in which the site can be revisited to learn what lies beneath the surface. More skulls, more carvings, more tools? Maybe humans can gain understanding that will help explain this world in which we live. As it is, it's the single most intriguing archaeological site in the Americas from my point of view.

Bonnye Matthews

Bibliography Included at End

Part 1

The four men walked rapidly downhill through the valley toward the big lake. As he walked the tall old man, Itz, shouted out venomously again, "I curse you!" His extraordinarily deep voice alerted a short-faced bear a good distance away. Grazing animals looked up scanning the area unsure how to react. Burrowers retreated to their tunnels. Birds in the forest prepared to take flight. Monkey shrieks cut the air with objection. The bear hastily left the area heading north.

"You must do good on first try this time!" Itz shouted to Wing, his sixteen-year-old son. "You must do good! Everyone tires of your lousy spear throws. Even your practice is lousy. Last time! Last time on hunt you missed on first throw. Amor and me, we no let people go hungry. We good hunters. Good spear throwers. You lousy. Why you so lousy?" Itz didn't expect an answer. Nearby animals sought refuge at a distance.

Wing walked ahead of his father on the trail to the hunting ground, the words piercing his gut as the beak of a terror bird pierced the belly of its arrested prey. He imagined blood dripping from his father's mouth as it would drip from a terror bird's beak. He could imagine the frenzy of the clacking beak as it delighted in tossing food down its throat. He compared it to the way his father would shake his head. Wing's father seemed to delight in taunting him. He couldn't understand why. Wing thought it might help if he knew why his father did that. He was glad he couldn't see the man. Hearing him was enough. Wing had pulled forward his shoulders, elevating them as if for protection against the words. He was unaware of his defensive posture.

"You have nothing to say?" his father sneered. "You no good hunter. You no good tool maker. You make no children!" With great force Itz stamped his foot on the ground.

Amor, a husky twenty-four year old, and Zik, a tall, lanky twenty-six year old walked behind Itz. They hardly saw the beauty of the blue sky day. No rain cleaned the air now that the dry time had come. The earth greened and wildlife was abundant. They had to hunt but hated the way Itz spoiled what could have been great fellowship. Amor and Zik preferred to hunt with the elder, Mig. They found it difficult to respect Itz when he mistreated Wing. They were required to respect their elders. Mostly they respected Itz, but when he treated Wing badly, they tried to say to themselves that they respected the man but didn't like him. That's what they were taught. It was awkward. At those times Amor argued with himself. Respect a man you don't like? He thought that was impossible and reasoned that he could not separate himself from himself and live. Amor admitted he sometimes hated his father for the way he treated this brother. Fortunately, Itz only did that when they went hunting. Otherwise Itz hardly recognized Wing's presence.

Itz knew Wing was sixteen years old. He also knew Wing was significantly short for his age. In addition Wing looked frail. Itz thought of him as female, but he would never say that, for it could reflect on him for producing a male that looked female.

"No good! You nothing but no good!" Itz spat the words at Wing. The old man's deep voice resonated through the forest. Itz moved forward and sharply hatcheted a blow to Wing's right arm.

Wing shuddered but uttered no sound nor put forth any effort to retaliate.

"You have nothing to say?" his father sneered. "You no good hunter. You no good tool maker. You make no children! You no even fight back!" Itz repeatedly stamped his feet on the ground—hard.

The ground shook violently beneath their feet. It lasted for a long time. Clearly it frightened Itz. Despite his pain, Wing smiled for the first time that day. Even the earth didn't like being stamped on. It shook back. Hard. Wing wondered how he might shake back.

As soon as he entered the shadow of the forest, Itz became silent. On the branches of an oak tree large parrots, having returned from their flight, quietly gazed down on the men as they moved silently on the path. Monkeys, making high-pitched chattering noises, scampered to the far side of the enormous tree.

A few camels stood in a small glen off to the left, their heads swiveled owl-like from time to time. Wing moved his spear from his left hand to the right. His upper right arm hurt. He'd felt and heard the bone crack. It hadn't broken all the way through, just cracked. It hurt to hold the spear. Wing moved stealthily while Amor and Zik moved up behind him. He reached a point within spear throwing distance. He raised his arm, creating shooting pain spears throughout his upper arm. He cast the spear and it fell short of the target. Amor and Zik hit the target and the camel went down.

"Well, your brother and cousin assure we eat tonight—again," Itz said, dripping condemnation with each word.

Wing stood there holding his upper arm, teeth clenched from the pain. His father's words were like the terror bird's kick at their prey after there was no longer anything left to devour. Rather than back up and walk around their devoured prey, terror birds would kick the prey to the side to unblock their own forward passage. Wing had seen it more than once. The throw had done additional damage to his arm. Wing felt tear darts leaving his eyes from the pain. He walked to the kill site, willing to help in any way he could, but the pain was almost unbearable.

Zik noticed Wing's pain. He quickly went to the forest and found two pieces of curved bark. He returned, and silently he felt Wing's upper arm bone, realizing it was a fracture not a break. Then he wrapped the arm with a piece of leather, wrapped the curved bark over the leather, and tied it well to provide support and reduce movement. Zik used cordage from the little bag on his side. It was his special cordage, but he didn't regret using it for this purpose. Toa, their grandmother, had made it when she could still see. Neither man spoke. Each knew it was best that way. When the splint was in place, each found their spears and placed them to the side while the men quietly butchered the camel. Afterwards they regathered their spears and carried the meat home.

After they ate that evening, Wing walked to the overlook where they had a great view of the whole valley. He pressed his fingertips against the center of his brow ridges. In the distance he could see a lion crossing the farthest point in the valley. It was alone.

Wing placed his left hand on his splinted arm. He thought of the male lion out in the world on its own. Lions did that. When they reached maturity, it was fight the old male lion or leave. And the idea struck. The spirits had given him a sign. He turned and went to the little cave where his family lived. He lay awake in the dark until his father was snoring. Then Wing gathered his spears and few things, rolled up his sleeping skins, and carefully left the only home he'd ever known. Wing would follow the valley past the place where they killed the camel and keep going. He'd go further southeast than ever before. He'd leave the land that trembled and shook hard, the land where smoke came from mountains. He'd find a new home. Somewhere there was a home not filled with pain. Wing determined to find it. Or he'd lose his life in the search. Like the male lion.

The moon was full and the night had a little crispness to it. Wing left the valley behind. He ached to leave his mother, brothers, and sister, but Wing was convinced he had to make this move. He wondered what life would be the next day and the days after. A crack off to the right alerted him. Wing stood completely still. His eyes scanned the area off to the right. Then he saw it. There was a jaguar moving through the brush. It was dragging something. He assumed correctly it was its nightly prey. Wing continued on more alert and more intent on walking silently.

When the sun reached its highest point of the day, Wing was in need of sleep. Some extremely shallow caves lined the hill on the left. He knew nothing about them, never having come this way on hunting trips. He climbed down the hillside and checked the caves. The largest one had no scent of animals and it offered shade from the sun, so he chose that one. He built a tiny hearth fire at the entryway. He laid out his skins and by the time he pulled the skin over his shoulder, he was asleep. When he awakened, he walked to the stream he'd been following and drank.

Wing noticed he'd been careless. He hadn't swept the cave. He now had a line of itchy spider bites across his abdomen. Wing had taken some camel pieces when he left home, and he ate part of his supply hungrily. He realized that, splinted arm and all, he had to plan to gather enough food to hold him until he could hunt well. His injured arm was his spear throwing arm. He grimaced at the complication.

Later that evening Wing looked about and found some onions. He wasn't far from an oak tree so he walked over and found acorns on the ground. They weren't in perfect condition, but he didn't care. Many times he'd eaten acorns with worms or some that were on the edge of rotting. He tried an acorn to determine whether it was too bitter to eat without soaking. He was pleased with the taste. He ate as many as he could find, until overfull. Wing scooped acorns onto a piece of leather which he tied into a bag. They'd be available food as he walked.

Not only had Wing walked carefully so as not to alert predators, but also he'd been careful to leave no tracks for others to follow. He intended to leave his home and would have been very unhappy to have been forcibly returned. So far it seemed that Wing had no followers. He gathered his few things and set out again. He was descending the lower southeast side of Popocatépetl. Wing traveled the animal trails near the forest edges, because he didn't want to be seen from above.

One evening after he'd been trekking for four full days, Wing sat on an outcrop and looked back to the north and then east. He was struck with the realization that he was out from under the shadow of Popocatépetl. In the evening at home, Wing mused, the mountain shaded his land when the sun began to set. In the late afternoons his people lived in the shadow of Popocatépetl. This land had more time with the light than his people had. For Wing it was a clarifying moment. His life had been under the shadow of Itz. Itz to him was like Popocatépetl to his people. As he felt the sun on his skin at this late part of the day, he was also free of his father's abuse. His arm had improved. There was only one problem. Wing was becoming terribly lonely.

Wing found a place for the night and set up some snares. He hoped to catch a small animal. A rabbit would suffice. He set up eight snares and established a small hearth to keep away predators at night in the open. Behind him for protection rose the trunk of a great evergreen tree. He slept well that night.

Wing arose the next morning with a new feeling for which he had no name. That feeling was freedom. He had lowered his shoulders and let his arms hang properly, not forced forward. He had no knowledge of the change in posture. In days the discomfort Wing felt from holding the defensive posture would decrease from the release on the muscles he'd unwittingly tightened. It was something that happened naturally and so gradually that it escaped his perception.

Wing checked the snares. He had managed to capture two rabbits. One was too small, so he freed it. He dispatched the adult quickly enough that it had little time to experience fright. He took it to his hearth, cleaned and skinned it, and prepared it to cook. Before long Wing had eaten and was busy putting out the fire, ready to continue his trek.

The day's trek was difficult. At times he had to climb down rock faces that were challenging. He was acutely aware that a fall could be lethal in this land where he was alone. He used caution that in other circumstances would have made him question his manhood. Alone here, it was necessary. Injury would be a luxury he couldn't afford. He already had a crack in the bone in his arm. A severe injury would require help from others. There were none. Where he'd normally drop four to six feet from a rock with ease, run across a fallen tree trunk, and swing from lianas, he chose his steps circumspectly, as if he were an elder.

Wing found a rockshelter that evening where he had an expansive view of the valley. Included in the view were tortured-looking mountains aligned roughly north to south with a bit of an arch bowing away from him. They appeared to have been painfully twisted by some irresistible force. Tortured? How could such a thing happen to land? For a moment he considered what happened to him could also happen to the land. Wing wondered at the mystery of it. He also found it strangely beautiful. It spoke of hope. The mountain was a mountain despite the torture.

Wing had gathered some pine nuts on his trek and at this place he located some greens. He ate plenty of both. He popped a few grubs he'd dug up into his mouth and chewed, savoring the bursts of liquid. Satiated, he settled down near the small hearth he'd made by the rockshelter. He watched as the light left the land, later than at home where the shadow of Popocatépetl darkened the land early.

Wing watched as an eagle came from the south and landed in a tree far below his view. For the creatures of the day it was time to sleep. He rested comfortably as stars began to appear in the sky. He slept before the stars became plentiful.

A golden mist gathered. It grew brighter and brighter. Wing became aware of the bright golden light. It grew in brightness, causing his sleep to lift.

He was more curious than frightened. He watched. The light moved nearer.

"Wing, son of Itz," a voice said slowly.

Wing was startled. Fear grew. He wondered how the man knew his name.

"Do not fear, Wing. I bring no harm."

Wing looked at the light. From the light an extraordinarily old man emerged. This man looked far older than his grandparents. Wing didn't know a face could hold so many wrinkles. He watched.

"You are to descend to the valley. Follow the valley southward many days. You will see an eagle perched on a pine nut tree. Watch. It will drop a feather. The eagle will leave. Look at the feather it drops. Don't touch it. Look at the feather's attachment point. That point directs you to the place you must go to the east. Follow the river to the mountain's crest. On the other side of the mountain there is another river. Follow that river to the salt water."

"Salt water?" Wing asked. "What is this salt water?"

"You used to hunt by the big lake. Salt water is many, many, many times larger than the big lake. Drink from rivers. Do not drink the salt water."

Wing was dumbfounded. Who was this man? From where had he come? What was the golden light? Why was this man telling him these things?

The man turned and walked back into the bright light. The light faded. The old man was gone.

The morning's sun warmed Wing's face. He opened his eyes, surprised to find the sun so high. He had slept longer than usual. He stretched and then remembered the bright light and the old man. He stood carefully, sweeping his gaze over the place where the man had stood. Since he'd stood in a place where Wing hadn't stepped, the young man tried to find evidence of the visit. From where he lay he could see no footprints. Vertical lines formed between Wing's eyebrows. Slowly and slightly cloudy of thought, he continued to stare at the place where footprints should be. He was careful not to step where the old man had. He inspected every part of the place where he anticipated finding footprints. He could find nothing. It made no sense.

"I must have been dreaming," he muttered, trying to dismiss the light and the old man.

Wing headed downhill to empty his bladder. He returned and mindlessly ate some pine nuts and greens. His hearth fire had gone out and he didn't want to start a new one to cook anything. He gathered his things and left the rockshelter, heading to the valley below at a faster rate than he had been using on the trek. The valley was very wide and open. Ungulates were grazing in large numbers, while others chewed their cud. He could hear the horses snort and saw one camel look up, alert to his presence. A sloth on the edge of the forest browsed the tops of trees. He knew that every animal in the area was aware of his presence, just as he was of theirs. All things were connected. Wing scanned the area carefully searching for animals that might consider him prey. He saw no cats, bears, terror birds, or wolves.

As he walked Wing considered the old man and the golden glow. Speaking to no one, he said aloud, "I must have dreamed it. The old man left no footprints. I remember going to sleep. I remember waking up. This had to happen at dream time." Wing chuckled. "I'm following the valley. He told me to follow the valley. To look for an eagle on a pine nut tree. A feather will point to the direction to salt water I cannot drink. Water not to drink? Strange dream. That's all it was. Just a strange dream. Tangled." He walked a little faster. "It's all a dream? I should be willing to go to the west or the north or to the south or east now. I feel compelled to follow this valley. Do I follow a dream?"

The ideas spooked Wing so he began to jog. He jogged for a long time. Finally, a little winded, he resumed the trekking. He stood still. Wing had seen a tiny movement in the trees. A parrot. The edge of his right eye had picked up the movement. He scanned the area until he was certain. Lying on the ground was a small peccary light in color around its neck. It appeared to doze. He considered how tasty that would be to eat that evening. He laid down his spears all except for his best. It was slender but very strong and went where he aimed it. Wing felt his arm was strong enough to thrust the spear with some force.

Wing crept up almost imperceptibly towards the peccary. How great it felt not to have someone undermining him all the way! That feeling again. That sense of freedom, a sense he didn't know existed until he moved from the shadow of Popocatépetl. He bared his teeth as he moved the spear backwards to increase the power of his thrust as it came forward. The spear flew straight and hit its mark perfectly. The little peccary was slain in a single spear throw.

"Why couldn't I do that in the presence of my father?" he asked aloud of no one.

Wing walked to the dead peccary, pulled out his spear, and picked up the animal. He carried it down the valley to a small stream. There he gutted and bled the animal. Wing carried the butchered pieces a good distance away and set up his camp for the evening. He slowly cooked the meat over a good sized fire, and while it cooked he made a lean-to just inside the border of the woods. One side protruded into the valley. It was near that side of the lean-to where he had the fire going. The smell of the meat cooking was causing Wing to salivate and occasionally saliva dripped from his mouth. It had been a while since he had meat this good. He intended to delight in this meal he'd single-handedly acquired.

As soon as the smallest meat pieces were ready, Wing took one and laid it on a large leaf he'd picked in the woods. He held it in place with a stick and cut off a piece which he then speared with the stick. He bit off a chunk, wincing a bit at the heat of the meat. It burned his lips.

Wing spent the evening gorging on the meat. He hadn't enjoyed food so much since the last time his mother cooked gomphothere. Thinking of the four-tusked elephant made him feel lonely again. He desperately missed his mother and brothers and sister. Only his two brothers, Amor and Spu, and one sister, Moot, remained at the only home he'd ever known. The rest had left long ago. He missed Zik and his parents, Mig and Koi, and Zik's brother, Aga, and sister, Lat. He also missed his grandparents, Puh and Toa. Wing wondered whether he'd ever see any of them again.

Wing reminded himself that he missed them because *he* left. He could not continue to take the abuse from his father. His emptiness was his own doing. And then he thought of the shadow of Popocatépetl. Wing smiled a wry smile. He would rather feel the emptiness and have that wonderful sense that had come to him. No abuse. Did he hunt better because he hadn't been abused beforehand? He was freed like the little rabbit he'd caught that was too small. Freed.

He tied up the meat and hung it from a tree nearby. If a bear were drawn to it, he didn't want to have to defend it up close. At a distance a bear might leave him alone.

It was a warm evening. Wing went to the nearby creek. He removed the leather skirt he wore and the leather cord around his neck where he'd tied the eagle claw he'd found. Apparently two eagles had misjudged their mating dive and died on a ragged piece of rock outcropping. He had treasured the keepsake, having no clue what meaning he derived from it. He hung the cord around a tree branch. Wing simply found the eagle claw irresistible. With the little grease still on his fingers, he polished the nails on each talon and softened the yellow skin. Wing waded into the water and bathed, trying to avoid allowing the splint to become wet. The water felt wonderful. His skin felt as if it could breathe again. Wing rubbed some of the sand into his hair, careful to rinse it all out. He walked briskly back to camp where he increased the blaze on the fire, then gathered more wood. He tied his skirt back on, having dried off sufficiently to keep the soft leather from hardening.

Wing listened to the birds' night songs, the frogs chorusing near the pond across the valley, the monkeys struggling to settle down nearby in a tree or trees. All the while insects created sounds that blended into a cacophonous mixture with the others. The sky was alive with color. Wing absorbed the beauty of it. A star appeared here and there. Wing started to doze off and jumped, seemingly involuntarily as if to catch himself in a fall. He knew he wasn't falling. Staring at a lovely sky and drifting off to sleep was how he went to sleep the night he dreamed of the old man. He didn't want to dream of the old man again. It was somehow unnerving. Finally, Wing slept after admonishing himself not to dream of old men.

In the morning Wing built up the fire and cooked more of the peccary. It was just as good the second time, maybe better, he mused. He wrapped the meat and prepared to travel. The fire clearly out, he began the day's trek. At one point on the trek Wing counted eight snakes in one place. They were not all of the same type. Wing carefully avoided them. They ignored him.

On the far side of the valley, Wing saw a small mammoth herd eating grasses. One noticed him and trumpeted. They were special animals to him. He loved to watch their sense of family. The herds contained none like Itz. All seemed to care for each of the others. He'd seen mammoths cry when one of their family members died. They hung around for a few days, seeming to hope the family member might wake up. Wing remembered that eventually, the mammoths had given up.

In the valley Wing had the oppressive feeling he associated with the shadow of Popocatépetl. Darkness came earlier there. He found a convenient rockshelter for the night and set up his camp, starting with a fire. He fixed a raised stick to spear through the meat so he could turn it to warm it thoroughly. As it began to cook, Wing searched about for some greens. He found some along with onions and a scraggly prickly pear leaf, which made him laugh, since it was out of place in this grassy valley. Wing also found mafafa, a large leafed plant with a corm (tuber) that was a starchy vegetable he loved. He could carry two or three small corms in his hand, but he wrapped the vegetables in a couple of mafafa leaves. Back at his hearth, he took his cooking bag out, adding a mafafa corm, some greens, pieces of the prickly pear leaf, and onion. Wing laid one of the mafafa leaves on a nearby rock after brushing the grit from the rock. It would make a good place to put his food.

Wing was thrilled. This would be the best meal he'd had since leaving home. All this, and he'd had no supporting hunters. He sat with his back against the rock, viewing the valley and savoring the smell of his meat.

From the south a short faced bear had caught the scent of the meat. It raised up to assess the direction of the captivating aroma. Then with fierce intent and saliva dripping from its loose-lipped, gaping mouth it headed toward the attractant with great speed. It stopped a distance from the hearth. Wing had spotted it, and his mouth filled with a coppery taste. He wondered whether the bear would take his life and eat him. Slowly, he reached stealthily for his spears. He stood. With a spear in each hand he held his arms out from his body. He began rhythmically moving his arms up and down, making his body look wider and taller than it was. He made no sound.

The bear looked at this strange creature moving without apparent fear. It stood clicking its teeth, saliva dripping down in a frothy mixture. The bear did have fear. It wanted the meat that drew him. He couldn't cease to fixate. Neither could Wing. He had hunted the peccary. It would be good meat. He already knew it. The vegetables were almost ready. He could not give the bear the opportunity to steal from him. Not this meal. It was *his*.

Wing let out a long, chilling shout that arrested the bear's fixation on the meat. The bear stood tall and glared at the strange creature with the huge voice. Wing began to stomp loudly on the ground as he advanced toward the bear.

"Leave here now!" Wing shouted in a deep, rarely used voice. It resonated with no trace of a tight throat of fear. "Leave! Go to your home. You will not have my food!" He continued to advance, arms out moving up and down. "Go! I tell you—go!" The bear became uneasy. It wagged its head and clacked its teeth. Wing advanced more forcefully and shouted orders in the deepest, most command-filled voice he could, "Go, go, go, go, go! Leave here now! Go, go, go, go, go!" He increased the speed of his advance. He was more forceful than he'd ever been. He felt imbued with significantly greater size. He sensed he brushed against things too far away for him to have touched.

The bear turned and ran. It ran south far faster than it came to the place. The bear had been completely frightened. It had never seen such a thing. Suddenly, running from the strange creature was much more important than a free meal.

Wing stood there, caught between relief and terror. His hands shook. He didn't want to chance breaking his spear points, so he put the spears back against the stone wall, walking on shaky legs to do so. He slumped to the ground, leaning against the stones, momentarily forgetting his food. After a while he could feel his heart beat at a normal rhythm. He looked around.

"I freed me!" he shouted at the top of his voice. "Freed me! Freed—m. Freed—m!"

The new feeling he felt—out from the shadow of Popocatépetl had a name—freedom!

In the far distance now, the bear heard. He recognized the sound of that voice. He ran faster. Far away.

"I never lose freedom—now I have!" Wing vowed. His words flew out through the valley and returned to him.

He remembered the food and went over to it, laying out on the leaf a good portion of meat from which he cut a tiny piece. He popped it in his mouth and grinned. Wing used sticks to fish out some of the vegetables and sat beside the rock where the food was displayed. He speared a large cut of the meat and ate big bites from it, juice running unchecked down his arms. He hardly noticed. Never had meat tasted so good. He speared a piece of mafafa corm. It was tasty. For the first time in his life Wing felt invincible. Like Popocatépetl. He was capable, strong, able to care for his needs and defend himself. His father was an elder, he realized, but his father was wrong about this son. Wing wasn't no good. Not at all! Truth wrapped its arms about Wing.

Wing went back for more food. He ate all the vegetables and a good portion of the meat. He nibbled on the leaf on which he'd put his food, particularly the part under where the meat had been. The leaf had picked up a little grit, but that was normal. He didn't notice. Then he put the remains of the leaf on the logs which were burning. Wing lay back on the ground, his hands behind his head. He had no desire for sleep. He kept whispering the word *freedom*. He toyed with it, savored it, wrapped himself in its meaning.

Wing rested on his sleeping skins. "I learned how to shake back!" he said aloud. "The earth shook back to my father's stomping. I just shook back to a bear. I know how to shake back!" Wing grinned a slow, long-lasting grin.

He watched the stars appear. He watched them move through the sky. Finally, his eyes closed and did not reopen. Wing slept.

The next day he opened his eyes as soon as light fell across his eyelids. Wing saw the world differently. He wasn't overly pride filled. Instead he had matured almost overnight. He had believed his father's conviction that somehow he was less than others. Wing knew now he'd believed a lie. He was as capable as any man. He wasn't the most skilled, but he had sustained himself in the wilderness. Wing had confronted and held his own against a fierce bear. None of the people he knew had done that. None he knew had ever been this long alone in the wilderness. Wing knew how to respect elders. He had just learned to respect himself. It was a perception he'd never experienced.

Wing also had a new regard for his tools. He had always taken care of them, but now he would be even more careful. He'd avoid chipping the points or splintering the shaft and try even more carefully to aim for the best thrust to avoid breaking a point on bone. Yes, his spears had saved his life. No one had ever taught him to do what he did to frighten the bear. In asserting himself the action seemed to be something that brought a new birth. The assertion brought freedom which built confidence.

It took Wing a long time to put the fire out. He was patient and carried water from the creek in his cooking bag to cool the fire pit. Finally, able to stand on the spot, he decided the place had adequately cooled to leave.

Wing walked for three days. He was moderately successful finding food each day. It became easier as he continued to do it. Sometimes, he'd spontaneously shout at the top of his voice, "Freedom!"

The idea and the fact raced through him igniting a sense of joy that was new. Occasionally he'd race ahead and jump high, spears lifted above his head. He was glad no one could see him. To be unrestrained was delightful, but deep down inside, he longed for people. Wing speared a small horse and enjoyed it before he slept that night in a comfortable rockshelter.

Wing opened his eyes to rain. It wasn't the season for rain. He didn't want his splint wet. He knew that he'd need it for a long time and was not able to secure it again, if he had to remove it. He had enough food from the small horse he'd speared the day before. Wing decided to wait out the rain. He did take a piece of leather that he used as a cloak when the weather chilled. He wrapped it around his shoulders and set out to find some greens or other vegetables to accompany the horse meat.

He walked south and noticed a pine nut tree in the valley, ran towards it, and came to a complete stop. There was an eagle sitting in the tree. Wing stood there in the rain completely dumbfounded. Rain trickled across his brow ridges and dripped to his chest. He didn't notice. A feather dropped from the eagle. Wing drifted back in time to the golden light and the old man.

The eagle made a great flapping of its wings and took to the air leaving just above Wing's head. For a moment Wing thought the old man's face replaced the eagle's face. Wing stood still as a rock in the rain. Then he moved. The eagle feather was large. He put his head to the side near the ground, visually lined up the feather, and looked to see where the feather attached to the bird. It pointed across the valley to a V in the hills. It was as if the V called him. Wing knew when the rain abated, he'd follow the directions of the old man. It made no sense, but he would follow the dream man when he could. He simply was unable to resist. In this he felt bound, not free. He finished searching for plants and returned to the rockshelter.

Part 2

After seemingly endless days of rain, the sun broke through and clouds scattered. Wing was convinced that it was a good time to travel. He gathered his things and walked south down the valley until he reached the tree where the eagle had left the feather. It still lay on the ground where he saw it. After a brief moment of indecision, Wing took the feather and placed it among his leather pieces. He looked toward the V across the valley and began to walk toward it. He crossed the mountain and began to go down the other side. It didn't take long for him to find the little creek that would lead to the river. From the mountain he could see that the ground sloped down to where it seemed to flatten. He saw nothing like a big lake. He concluded that the salt water must be at quite some distance.

Wing stood atop the small mountain. A good hearty laugh broke forth from its pit of long incarceration, a slightly twisted laugh, not one of joy—but a laugh nevertheless. He held his arms out to the side. "I am standing here looking for salt water in the distance because I dreamed it!" He had no confidence in dreams. None whatever. Wing considered dreams as tangled thoughts, tangled as cordage sometimes tangled, having nothing to do with his real life or how things should be. Yet the compulsion to continue on down to the little creek so he could follow it was irresistible. "I have turned my thoughts over to an ancient man who appeared in a dream," he muttered while walking downhill. Wing laughed aloud again, not bitter this time, more from surprise at himself but leaving self-condemnation behind.

As Wing approached the broken lands of the piedmont, he heard a man's voice. He stood still and listened. As lonely as he'd become, he was not sure it would be wise to enter quickly into land where others lived. Wing looked for a place where he could observe without being seen. He chose a point of land that had a moderately adequate rockshelter. Using every safety measure he knew, Wing carried his things there. He crept out on the point and was just barely able to see the little place below where people had built tiny dwellings and covered them with grasses. Trees blocked his full view. There was open land where grass did not grow well all around the little dwellings. Children played. There seemed to be several children. There were more people compared to the number that remained at his homeland. From where he watched, adults were the size of his longest fingernail on an outstretched arm. Wing stood no chance of survival if these people saw him as violating their place. He knew he must be careful. He would make no fire.

Finally, after days of solitude, Wing could tolerate the loneliness no longer. He built a small fire at the land's end of the point. Contact did not take long. Three very tall men came to his camp. Their spears were substantial. Wing walked to meet them showing no fear. He'd already accepted the fact that the meeting would be what it would be.

The three men talked among themselves as they looked at Wing. At first Wing was disappointed. He could not understand them. Then suddenly he realized they spoke his language only with slightly different pronunciations of the words. They also didn't talk as fast.

Wing pointed to himself. "I am Wing." He said it slowly and carefully.

The tall man with graying hair said, "Wing. I am Bort, son of Puh. The next man said, "I am Miger, Son of Bort." The third man said, "I am Hama, son of Bort."

Wing looked at them for a long time before speaking. Then he said, "My grandfather is Puh. My grandmother's name is Toa."

The tall man stared as if to drill a hole through Wing. "Then you are my brother's child. Which brother?"

Wing stared at the ground. "Itz," he said quietly.

43

"I didn't like Itz," Bort admitted. "He was mean spirited. Did he do that?" the man asked, pointing to Wing's arm.

Wing nodded, feeling shame.

"Come," Bort said, "You have a new place here. You stay as long as you want." Bort walked over to Wing and embraced him.

Wing burst into tears. He was infuriated at his reaction, but he couldn't hold back any longer.

The three men encircled Wing, placing the palms of their hands on his upper body. "You are one of us now. Have no fear. You are one of us. You will find little groups of Puh's children all across this land. When you meet people be sure to say you are Wing, son of Itz, son of Puh. You will be accepted by everyone from here to the salt water. Let's gather your things."

Wing composed himself. He gathered his things and followed the men down to the little village. As they walked he asked, "What is the salt water?"

"Coming from the Popocatépetl area you wouldn't know. You've seen the big lake. The big lake is like a raindrop. The salt water is like as many big lakes as you have fingers and thumbs—or more."

Wing let that information settle. It was so utterly astounding that he could not make a place for it in his understanding.

As they approached the village people came towards them to see the stranger. Bort put his hand on Wing's left shoulder. He looked into Wing's eyes and said, "We will talk later. I want Topozelmu to look at your arm." To the people Bort said, "This is Wing, son of Itz, son of Puh."

Instantly the people understood the connection and welcomed the young man. He was family and to be respected.

Wing walked into the crowd of people led by Bort.

"Where's Topozelmu?" Bort asked.

"Here!" came the reply. She came at a run.

"Take this cousin and look at his arm." Then he asked, "Do you have room for him in your hut?" She nodded. Of course Bort knew she had room. Topozelmu guessed he had more in mind than nursing an injured arm. Bort would also know she wouldn't object, even if she didn't want to share her hut yet. Topozelmu realized with a slight surprise that she had no objection. She nodded a second time to Bort in agreement.

Bort left Wing to Topozelmu. She led him to a quiet place where curious people stood around but gave great space in front of the hut where Topozelmu led him.

"Is it fully broken?" she asked.

"No, just a line break." Wing was gratified the woman was so kind. She was gentle as she removed the splint. Her voice was quiet and melodious, a combination he'd never heard. She washed the arm and felt it carefully. He was sure she missed nothing.

Wing was grateful she didn't ask how the injury occurred. What he didn't know is that she knew about Itz. She knew Itz could be very mean spirited and violent. Itz had many children. Most left the area as soon as possible. Wing wasn't the first to leave. He was definitely the youngest in her awareness. Most of those who left were well into their twenties and were seasoned hunters. Most left in twos or threes. She knew of none having left alone until Wing.

As Topozelmu replaced the splint with leather and wood, Dah came over and sat beside Wing.

"I'm Dah, son of Miger, son of Bort."

Wing looked at him expectantly.

"I have lived twenty-one years. You?"

"Sixteen."

"I will show you this land," Dah said. "It's good land. I've never seen your land. I have heard about it. You can see Popocatépetl from here. Only when no clouds. This land is piedmont land. It's the bottom part of the mountains. Piedmont is between the great mountains and the flat land. Flat land goes to the salt water."

"Is there a difference in the animal life here?" Wing asked as he picked up the cordage Topozelmu had discarded. He knew the cordage was special to Zik and that Toa had made it. Wing hoped someday to return it to Zik.

"My father, Miger, says more bears and wolves near big lake. We have more terror birds. Here we have many camels, deer, horses—mammoths too. Plenty rabbits, turtles, peccaries. You good hunter?"

"Not very good. I managed to feed myself through the wilderness."

"I would not want to depend on myself to cross the wilderness. You have encounters with wolves, bears, or terror birds while traveling?" Dah asked.

Wing nodded.

"Which of them?"

Wing looked up. "Bear."

"You had to stand up to bear?" Dah was awestruck.

Wing nodded, remembering.

"You will tell story tonight?" Dah asked, eager to hear it.

"If people wish to hear," Wing agreed.

Dah excused himself and went off fast. He found Bort and told him Wing had an experience with a bear and was willing to share.

After Dah left, Eku, Dah's youngest sister came over to see Wing.

"How'd you hurt your arm?" she asked quietly. Eku was six years old. Her brown eyes sparkled and her straight, black hair shone in the light. Wing was fascinated with her long, thick eyelashes.

"That's a story for another day," he replied.

Eku looked surprised. "It's a long story?" she asked.

"Yes, it's a long story," he assured her. "What's your name?"

"I'm Eku, daughter of Miger, daughter of Bort. I already know who you are. You lived on the white-topped mountain. The mountain that smokes. That's amazing."

Wing had to stifle a chuckle. It never struck him as amazing to live on the mountain. Off to the side, Topozelmu was making the same effort to disguise her amusement. She knew Eku loved expressive words.

"It's a beautiful place to live," he said.

"Then, why you leave?" she asked.

"Well, Eku, beauty is only one part of a choice of where to live."

"This is a beautiful place to live. Was it like this?"

"A little different. The land slopes a lot. There are many more forests. The land without trees is mostly covered with grasses."

"I see," she said studiously.

Wing was concealing his desire to laugh out loud. He discovered quickly that he dared not look at Topozelmu.

Eku looked at Wing's chest. She reached out and cradled the eagle foot in her hand. "Wing, why you wear this? Should it be on the dirt? Might it want to go back to eagle land?"

Wing laughed out loud. "Eku, you're a special one." He hugged her. "I found it one day when I wandered the rocky hills. Mating eagles dive to the ground together. Just before hitting the ground they fly up. This pair didn't make it. They hit the rock and broke apart. I don't know why I found this important. I just did."

"You take good care of it."

"I try, Eku. Now, I have some things I must do. You need to leave me. I see you later." He went to place his things in Topozelmu's hut. He desperately needed to relieve himself.

Eku showed her disappointment, but she didn't speak of it. "Yes, Wing. I go now." She stood up and walked away. She had her mind on the eagles that dived down to earth and split apart on the rocks. She thought eagles were not thinking well to do something so foolish. They threw away life for no reason she could see.

People began to bring food and place it on a fallen log. Wing couldn't believe the variety of food. There were vegetables, nuts, and fruit there he'd never seen. He began to realize how hungry he was. He hoped his eagerness for food wasn't too obvious. He had contributed nothing.

Bort called the people to eat. Topozelmu led Wing to the line. She handed him a plate of wood to hold his food. Wing wasn't shy. When he wondered what a specific food was, he asked and she explained. He tried numbers of things he'd never tasted. Wing couldn't believe his good fortune to find people who treated him so well. He did have a strange compulsion to continue to the salt water, but thought he should wait until his arm healed. He ate and enjoyed everything.

After the food was eaten and put away, the group gathered in a place to the north where the land was flat. Slabs of rock had been placed on the ground for seating. The sun was setting. A bit of a cool breeze drifted through the village. Wing marveled at how people treated each other.

Eku walked over and asked if she could sit with Wing. Her mother reached for her, but Wing demurred. "She's fine," he said as Eku climbed over his leg to sit on it, as if his leg were a fallen tree. His shock made Eku's mother chuckle, but she left her daughter to Wing.

There was group singing, something Wing had never experienced. Hunters shared information they learned that day. Then Bort said, "Wing has had an experience with a bear. Let us listen to him. He will share the story with us."

Wing sat a little straighter. Eku twisted so she could look up at his face. He rested his hand gently on her shoulder.

"On the trip there is a long valley. I had a good shot at a peccary. My arm is not good for hunting. I managed to kill the peccary on the first spear throw. I was so happy. I knew I'd eat well. I relaxed while the meat cooked. I enjoyed it. The next evening after trekking all day, I found mafafa and onions to eat with the meat. I began to cook it. Suddenly a short faced bear came running toward the hearth. Now, I wanted the meat. I really wanted it. I didn't want bear to kill me. It was my meat. You know that feel?" He paused looking at the hunters. "I took both my sticks." He slid Eku from his lap. Wing picked up two sticks on the ground. His spears were in Topozelmu's hut. He stood. "I stood there and held the spears out. Like this." He held his arms straight out to the side. "I began to raise them and lower them. I wanted the bear to think I was big. I felt big. Much bigger than I am." Wing kept moving the sticks rhythmically as he'd done. "The bear didn't know what to think. It kept looking at my meat. Suddenly I began to shout at the bear to go. I used my deepest voice. I was forceful." He demonstrated while moving the spears. He felt he was reliving the experience. "I think forcefulness important. It shifted bear's attention from the meat to me. I stomped the ground and yelled at the bear. I moved toward it with strong purpose." He demonstrated.

For a moment as he relived the charge he made, he was transformed in the eyes of the people. They could envision the young man transformed into a fierce threat to the bear. "For some reason, I frightened the bear. It turned and ran away fast."

All around murmurs rose: "Well done." "I'd never have thought of that!" "Good hunter!" The comments continued. All positive.

Wing had never been complimented. He blushed, his neck and cheeks becoming almost sunset red.

Bort walked over to Wing. He placed his hand on Wing's shoulder. "Well done, Wing. You taught us something tonight." He sat down nearby. "Wing, what made you think to make yourself look bigger?"

"I do not know. Something happened. I decided the bear could not have my food. A change took place in me. I suddenly knew what to do. It wasn't thought out. It just came to me. Could it have been help from the ancestors? Could they have filled me with knowledge?"

"Wing, we'll talk more on this tomorrow. You have given us food for our thoughts not bellies. You may have saved a life tonight. A man could frighten a bear! You lost your fear."

"I've thought about that. I think it had to do with anger. I controlled anger. Controlled anger became useful. Let me share something about my father. He treated me badly. He wanted a son different from me. I could only be me. My father gave me a hard time. He spoke discouraging words to me and about me. One day he was angry and stomped his feet violently. When he did, Popocatépetl and all the land around shook hard.

I thought about that. I wanted to learn to shake hard when things were wrong. Then the bear thought to take my food. I judged that as wrong. I wanted to shake back. I became stronger than myself. Something filled me. I made the bear fear me. I was willing to die to keep the bear from my food. And then I had no fear. I learned to shake back. It gave me something. I call it *freedom*. You can free a too young rabbit from a snare. I thought of myself freed. That's the loss of fear. I was freed from fear of the bear. I thought of it as *freed me* or *freed—m* and named it freedom. It's freed from fear. You're different then. Stronger. Sure. Frightening to bears." Wing had never said so many words at one time in his life.

The hunters were electrified. Here was a frail looking small sixteen year old. Hardly a man yet. He had learned to control fear and defeat a bear alone. They were astonished. They had learned much.

Bort stood. He addressed the people, "We have learned much tonight. Let us go now to our huts. Let us think on this new understanding. Thank you, Wing. Thank you."

"You're welcome," Wing said quietly.

Wing and Topozelmu headed toward her hut.

"Why you live alone, Topozelmu?" Wing asked as they walked to her hut.

She lowered her head. "I was Tupo's wife. We loved very strong. He was hunting. A bear killed him, Wing. Your story tonight. I wish he'd heard story before . . .." Her voice trailed off.

Wing wished he hadn't asked.

"Come," she said, "This is your place. Skins are good. It is comfortable."

"Thank you, Topozelmu. You are kind."

"You are welcome in my hut."

Wing barely pulled the skin over his shoulder before he was asleep. He could not believe how wonderful these people were. He enjoyed being with them and wanted to remain with them, but there was a compulsion to go to the salt water. He'd wait until his arm healed.

In another hut Bort sat by a small hearth. Veza looked at him. "He doesn't understand," she said flatly.

"No, he doesn't. He needs to learn. He must not fail to honor the spirit." Bort covered his face with his hands. Big knuckles grew misshapen causing his fingers to curve somewhat grotesquely across his forehead and brow ridges.

Veza looked at Bort's body expression. She ached for him.

At the first meal of the day Dah found Wing and suggested they explore the area so Wing could learn his surroundings. Bort walked over to the two and said, "Wing before you do anything else this day, we need to talk. We will return to the place we found you yesterday."

Wing and Dah were surprised. Wing put away left over food he had not consumed and went to Topozelmu's hut to pick up two of his spears. He found Bort and wordlessly the two left the village area. Veza watched the two leave. She busied herself quickly in caring for the remains of the food.

When they reached the place overlooking the village, Bort and Wing sat on the large rock. A slight sweet fragrance passed by on the breeze.

"Why we here? You must wonder. I explain," Bort said.

Wing nodded.

"You meet stranger. He and you different?"

Wing's thoughts raced. He wondered what the man meant. Surely he didn't mean the man in the dream?

"You did? Yes?"

"You mean a real person? Not a dream."

"It could be a dream."

"I had a dream. The oldest man appeared from a golden mist in the dream. I never saw such an old man. Next day I found no footprints. He told me to go to a pine nut tree down valley. I'd see eagle. The eagle would lose a feather. The tip would point to a V in the hills. I should go there. He said something odd. I should not touch feather. I saw where it pointed. Then it rained. I ran to my shelter. I stayed there for days in rain. Then rain stopped. I went back to tree. I put feather in with my leather things. I followed the trail the feather showed me. It brought me here."

"You met a spirit." Bort was resigned to initiating the young man.

"Spirit? You can't see spirits!" Wing was shocked. His thoughts swirled.

"Sometimes they make themselves seen."

"They can do that?"

"Yes. Once spirit talks, you listen for rest of your life." Bort's words came slowly.

"What?" Wing didn't understand.

"Spirit talks to me. I know he there all days all through day. I must do what he say."

"You're talking about a real spirit. This is not child story?"

Bort laughed a genuine laugh that released a little tension.

"No. Not a child story. There is reason for all of us to be born. Some know and do their purpose. No one need tell them. Some need more guidance. They have to do some things required in the plan of things. They must understand it right. You and I are both ones who need to be told." Bort relaxed. He'd said what he knew he had to say.

"Someone like Topozelmu reasons better?" Wing asked quietly.

Again Bort laughed, releasing more stress.

"I had a son. I loved the son. He the first son. Name Pote. Sprit talked to him too. Pote was not interested. He ignored spirit. He told me about his encounter with spirit. He shared his responses. Spirit say do this. Pote do opposite. Not wise. Pote's contempt for spirit frightened me. Spirit say Pote will stay home this day. Pote went to meet girl from another village. Lightning from sky touched him. Pote died. Girl saw. She terrified. She told me." A tear slid down Bort's face.

"Sorry you lost son, Bort."

"I, too."

"I like you, Wing. I want you listen. You must obey spirit. Your life depends. You understand?"

"I do understand. I will obey."

"Spirit know disobedience. You understand?"

"I cannot hide from spirit?"

"That right. You understand."

"I must go to the salt water. Not say when. Just say go." Wing shared the spirit's message.

"Spirit told you?"

Wing nodded.

"Then, we help you go there. You want others go with you?"

"I would be grateful." Wing's enthusiasm and relief showed clearly.

"The soonest you go is tomorrow."

Wing was startled. He had thought he'd be at the village until his arm healed.

"I send Dah, Hama, and Topozelmu with you."

"A girl?" Wing asked, then lowered his head thinking he might have offended.

"I send Topozelmu for arm care. Dah and Hama know nothing about healing."

"I understand." Wing was amazed at Bort's kindness. He smiled.

"Wing, in our village girls hunt."

"Girls hunt?" Wing was stupefied.

"Yes. They also good in fight with other people."

"Girls fight?" Wing could not believe what he was hearing. Girls did not hunt or fight in his home.

"Girls fighting may surprise you. They don't fight in the village of Puh. I know. In our village we want everyone prepared. Topozelmu is excellent hunter. Stealthy as jaguar. Aim true."

The earth shook with surprising violence. It was over quickly.

"Why so much shaking?" Wing asked, concerned since he'd noticed a definite increase in earthquakes.

"Earth just making changes. Changes often. Not to fear. Sometimes great damage. Sometimes none. We repair great damage. We die from earth change? We no worry about repair then. We happy in life after."

"Life after?"

"Life after this one, Wing. When we become spirit life in spirit land for people."

"How you know that?" Wing asked. He was learning so fast he could hardly keep up.

"Spirit man you met. You will talk again. They tell you things. You can ask. Sometimes they answer."

"Is the spirit man one? Are there many of them?" Wing asked.

"I talk to wrinkled old man. I never discuss what you asked. Your wrinkled old man may be my wrinkled old man. Could be only one. Could be more." Bort was surprised that he was learning things from Wing. Last night about frightening bears, today questions about number of spirits or just one.

"This talk good. I learn much," Wing said.

"Remember, obey the spirit," Bort insisted, "Now, we go back to village. We prepare for tomorrow."

They stood and left for the village. Wing stood a little straighter. He wondered at all the changes since he'd left home. He had learned so much so fast and wondered what purpose the salt water held for him.

Dah came up to them as they arrived back in the village.

"Dah," Bort said. "This is important. Wing must go to salt water. This spirit say. I want you and Hama to join him. Topozelmu go. She care for Wing's arm."

"I go to prepare," Dah said quickly. To Wing he explained, "We explore this area some other day. Other day when return."

The village heard the news of the trip planned by the newcomer and three of their own. They busily prepared what would be needed for a group of four to the salt water. People required no guidance. They knew exactly what was necessary and those of thirteen years or more were busy contributing to a successful trip. They gathered tools, leathers for many reasons, cordage, food, dried mosses, herbs, strong healing pastes, dried meat, vegetables, and fruit. Hama loved to carve, so they tossed in a few pieces of bone to occupy his time. By time for sleep the packs were prepared and ready for the next morning.

Bort saw them off with the following cryptic remark: "Stay at the salt water cave at least three days."

"The one near the hill or the one near the lake?" Dah asked.

"The one on the hill," Bort said. "The one near the lake isn't really a cave."

Dah thought about that, and then nodded at his father. He was right, of course. It was more of a shelter under a strange rock.

Wing, Dah, Hama, and Topozelmu left. No one questioned Bort's remark. They respected the elder. For all he said, he had reason, even if they didn't know it. Each trekker was burdened with a roll that had ties they could put over their shoulders and tie to a band at their waist in front. All chose to tie the burden on so their arms were free. Each carried multiple spears. Additional spear heads were placed carefully in packs.

Wing was delighted to be accompanied. Not only was the accompaniment welcome, but also they knew where they were going.

For days they traveled downward. Each day when the weather was clear Wing could see the flat land coming closer. He thought it would be much easier to walk on the flat land.

They had descended to such an extent one day that Wing noticed he could no longer see the tip of Popocatépetl. It was a clear day. He was surprised that the mountain was no longer in view. He wondered how long it had been hidden by the mountains he'd descended. He asked Dah about it.

"Ask Hama," Dah told him.

Hama smoothed the dust and showed him how a line from their place to the top of Popocatépetl was interrupted by the top of the mountains they were on. Mountains shorter than Popocatépetl. Wing was fascinated. He'd never seen anyone draw anything. He understood immediately and it seemed so simple. He was overwhelmed at the knowledge of these people. His people had not questioned things and sought answers as these people did. It was such a difference. He was part of something exciting and new. He was filled with joy to think that they were also his people through Puh. He tried to think that his people back on Popocatépetl could be like this. Then, he realized sadly that it was impossible. Itz had too much power. The idea of a woman hunting or fighting would be quashed by Itz in a breath. He didn't like women much. Itz saw women as makers of food and babies—nothing more.

When they stopped the first night, they stayed at a rock shelter they'd known from their former journeys to the salt water. They went to the salt water often enough that the journey was very familiar. Dah and Wing left the shelter to hunt. Dah speared a small camel. They hung it to bleed and skinned it away from the shelter. They quartered it and carried the pieces back to their hearth. They put three of the pieces in a small lake and submerged them, placing rocks on top to keep them submerged. Topozelmu and Hama were busy preparing to cook the meat they were certain would be forthcoming. To make it quick, they had made spears that would secure small pieces of meat each individual could hold over the fire. Small amounts of fruit and vegetables accompanied each leaf for each person. They'd eat well.

Dah and Wing washed off at the lake and came to eat. As the sun set, they circled the hearth and held their spears over the fire. They ate the fruit and vegetables while they cooked the meat, having placed their leaves in front of them. Night noises began to surround them. Dah, Topozelmu, and Wing chatted. Hama had taken a piece of mammoth bone and begun to carve lines into it using the fire to see. Bugs and tree frogs were especially loud outside. In the distance a trumpeting noise waved through the din. Hama thought it was a four-tusked gomphothere and decided he'd carve one on the bone. Finally, despite the noise, they settled to sleep.

It took many days to reach the flat land. It was different from anything Wing found familiar. There were more snakes in this place and some of the land was marshy. Wing was fascinated to learn about tidewater. He knew mountains. He'd learned piedmont as a form of the land. Now this land was described as tidewater because twice a day the water rose in the rivers. Wing found it incomprehensible. On flat land, the tide could cause the river to rise because the salt water rose. He also learned that rivers have a salty taste when one reaches a certain part of the river and that the people had a place on the river where the water was good.

He learned that when Dah and Hama gathered numbers of bladders and filled them with good water. They had to carry water to the salt water so they did not thirst after they arrived. They had something called a boat that they used to travel to the salt water. The first time Wing saw the salt water he was dumbstruck. The salt water covered such a great area, extending from the north to the south. Standing on a projection of sand, he felt surrounded by the salt water, and he wanted to reject what he saw, but he was unable, for it was there. He'd thought views from tall mountains were the largest of all vistas. The salt water seemed infinite. That word, infinite, did not reside in his vocabulary. Instead, he felt it. The water was too immense for his comfort. The enormity of it frightened him. He would not want to be out on that water. He preferred the forests where a tree could provide protection from an angry animal or a terrible wind. Rivers and lakes provided protective banks. He saw no protection on the salt water.

"Today we take the boat," Dah told Wing as they ate. The boat was eight trees from which the limbs were removed. They were held together in the form of a raft. Dah and Hama would take turns steering the boat from the rear and poling it from nearer the front. "You must sit in the center and keep your arms and legs close to the center. There are big lizard-like animals here. We call them alligators. They are big enough to eat you. They are as long as half the length of our village."

"Surely you tease me," Wing said quietly with a part smile. Since they'd become better acquainted on the trek, there had been some teasing.

"No, he's not teasing," Topozelmu assured him. "Watch the edges of the river. You'll start to see them now. They live where warm. Not like shadows in mountain forests. You find them by rivers and lakes and ponds. They are mean beasts and always hungry. There, look over there. See on the river's side?

"I can hardly believe it. That thing is huge and ugly! It's frightening." Wing had ceased to wonder what else there was to learn about this land.

"Good reason to keep your arms and legs to the center of the boat."

They followed the river for three days and finally arrived at the mouth where it entered the eastern salt water. On the north side of the river the land rose as a formidable hill. It was there where a great cave followed the land back and provided an excellent shelter. They beached the boat and headed toward the salt water cave. The cave was on a hill high above water level. Inside the floor was soft sand. Wing stretched out on the sand for a moment. It was cool and soothing to his sunburned back. Beyond the opening the cave had an expansive view of the beach and water.

Wing was delighted with the cave. He was pleased to be out from the sun. His skin had been protected by forests all his life. The sun had made his skin blister and it was peeling. It didn't feel good. He was tired.

"Bort mentioned this cave to stay three days?" Wing asked, carrying two of the water bags.

"Yes. This is it." Hama assured him. We like this cave. It shows the water well. Bring the last piece of the deer and waterbird, Wing. We will eat those tonight. We hunt tomorrow."

Wing gathered the meat and carried the burden to the cave. Topozelmu had already set up the roasting sticks preparing for the meat.

Hama had taken a roll of leather and was busy sweeping the sand from four rocks that formed an arc at the hearth. Wing would soon understand they were places for seating. Their rolls were on the highest point in the cave, more than thirty feet above the level of the water.

"I don't like the look of the clouds," Dah said. "We must stay three days. A big storm comes."

Wing walked outside of the cave. He noticed a cloud that arched out from him, but there was nothing to alert him to danger of any kind. The cloud looked normal to him.

Hama went out and surveyed the sky. "Yes, Dah, it's going to storm. Three days. We do three days. We should look to the boat. It may need better securing. Maybe tie to tree down there?" He pointed.

"I'll take care of it," Dah said and headed toward the boat.

They ate that evening looking at a beautiful view of the salt water. The full moon rose and made a path like line of whitish gold splotches on the waves. Wing was absorbed into the beauty of the place. Hama took out his knife and mammoth bone. Topozelmu removed the splint on Wing's arm. She washed the arm and replaced the splint.

"Wing, you've seen storms. The one that will come here is greater. Compare the big lake to the salt water. Make that comparison with storms you know and this one. This one is like the salt water."

Wing looked at her with a feeling of horror. "Why we stay then?"

"Bort said stay three days. We'll find out why in time. Right now we do it. We see why later."

"Isn't this dangerous?" Wing asked.

Hama looked up from his work. "Life dangerous," he said laconically.

"More dangerous to defy spirit," Dah said.

Wing flew back in time to the description of Bort's son killed by lightning.

Dah said, "Defy spirit. You become burnt by lightning. You heap of charcoal."

No wonder, Wing thought, that Bort agonized over his son. To look at a son as a heap of charcoal would be devastating. Such a visual would be impossible to forget.

They sat on the rocks to eat. The deer meat was very tasty. They enjoyed it after the day's travel. They were quiet. The salt water background noise instead of forest fauna background noise consisted of waves crashing on the shore. When it was daylight, sea bird noise accompanied crashing waves. Wing inhaled deeply the salted moisture. It made him feel a gentle calm.

"I think we have enough strong cordage," Topozelmu said.

Wing wondered what the point of the statement was. He didn't ask.

"I checked already," Hama said. "We have more than enough. Your shoulders should have told you that. We had heavy packs to carry. Heavier than usual."

"What are you talking about?" Wing finally asked, completely mystified.

"Oh, in storms if we have to go out, we tie ourselves together. It keeps a single person from being blown away. The winds can carry you away."

"This storm must be fierce. Why so fierce here, not back where we were?"

"It comes strong from water. We think land slows it down and it turns storm into more of huge rainstorm. Trees protect village," Dah explained.

"I see," Wing said.

Wing may have thought he had some understanding of what was to come. The beginning of the third day the storm was blowing. The sky was pitch black and charcoal with bits of gray and white—frightening with winds howling piteous noises. Wing was intimidated, never having seen anything like it. Here he was far from home, looking at salt water that was of immeasurable size, being set upon by a storm that made it hard to hear. He was grateful for the cave. It protected them from the wind and some of the noise. The water level was rising. Wing wondered whether it would enter the cave and they'd drown. He kept his fears to himself.

Wing felt a terrible sense of unease. He walked toward the cave entryway.

"Stop there!" Dah shouted. He ran over and took his foot and made a line in the sand. Do not cross that line," Dah said.

Wing looked startled.

"The wind can reach in and grab you. It will pull you out there. You'd be gone," Dah explained.

"I feel drawn," Wing tried to explain. "Something urges me. Can you not tie me and let me look out?"

"Is this some spirit thing?" Dah asked.

"I don't know," Wing replied.

Dah was not pleased, but he went to the back of the cave and brought out some strong cordage.

"I tie you to me. Hama holds cordage from me. We do this quickly."

Wing nodded. They tied themselves together.

Wing walked to the cave mouth. He stared into a churning sea. It was hard to understand what he saw. Then he thought he saw something on the water. It was dark. He wasn't sure he actually saw anything. "There, can you see that?" Wing asked Dah.

"I can't see anything," Dah said.

"You're not far enough out," Wing replied.

Dah and Hama tied themselves together. Then Hama and Topozelmu joined in cohesive strengthening links so that all four were secured together. Slowly Wing and Dah crept to the entryway, with Hama and Topozelmu serving as anchors. They stared into the dark water.

Dah wanted to turn around, until suddenly he saw something. He squinted.

"There it is," Wing said. "See it?"

Dah had to admit, "Yeah. I see it."

"What is it?" Wing asked.

"It looks like a boat," Dah said. "We watch it for a while."

They watched as the object was tossed about on the waves. A large wave caught it just right and hurled it much closer to shore. Hama and Topozelmu, neither of whom could see the object watched the bodies of Wing and Dah as they moved in reaction to the object.

"A man on the boat! See him?" Dah asked.

"Yes. Are there two?" Wing asked.

"Looks like two."

"It comes nearer. We may have to go out there." Dah realized they might need to save the man by letting him or them know where people were.

"Anyone unwilling to go out?" Dah asked.

Silence returned to him. He wished he were the lead on the line, but there was little time. The four went outside and walked a line on the beach as far up from the water as possible. They wanted to show their presence.

After what felt like a long time the man in the boat waved at them. The man's wave looked very tired.

Wing said something to Dah but immediately realized he couldn't be heard. They waved to the boat man.

The men on shore were dressed and their clothing was soaking wet. Fortunately they each had a change of clothing so they did not even concern themselves. Each was intently watching the man in the boat. As it neared the water's edge, they could see another person in the boat. That person was lying down and not moving.

Finally the boat met the water's edge and the people raced out to help. They gave a hand to the man who had waved. He stepped out of the boat and fell upon the beach. The other man was unconscious and cold to the touch, so they lifted him from the boat. They carried him to the cave and helped the other man walk there.

In the cave, the man who waved broke down in tears. Both men were starving. Their bones protruded in a horrifying manner. Topozelmu, assured herself that the second man lived, and she took some of the fish they'd put aside after eating and added it to water after cutting it into tiny pieces. She put it along with a tiny piece of a mafafa corm into a bag with water and added a number of herbs. She placed rocks from the fire into the bag and warmed the soup. Topozelmu put some of the soup in a gourd and handed it to the man who'd waved. He nodded his head in gratitude and took the offered gourd. She put broth into another gourd and went to the other man. Topozelmu used a stirring stick to drip little drops of the liquid into his mouth. Never had she seen anyone alive so thin. It caused her extreme discomfort. Her cursory examination showed starvation to be the major problem.

The people had only three spare sleeping skins. They decided to put the two men together so they could keep each other warm. They'd cover them with two skins. Dah showed the first man where to sleep. Then, Dah lifted the other man to a place on the sleeping skin. They were in position to gain warmth from the hearth fire. The others changed out of their wet clothing and unrolled their skins for the night.

Wing, readying for sleep and still having discomfort from the sunburn, considered based on the skin color of the men they rescued, they must have been badly burned. He didn't ask.

Topozelmu had no way to determine the passage of time, so she used the material in the fire. When she brought the fire back up, she'd make more of the fish soup. She'd feed both men the soup and then doze. She did that through the night and the next day.

Dah tried to communicate with them. It was a little difficult, but the one who waved, named Doeoi, was picking up their language fast. He was also eating. Careful not to overeat, he was doing better. His friend was not doing well at all, and he died the second day in the cave. They carried his body a good distance north of the cave and buried him. Doeoi was devastated. They'd gone through so much together.

On the evening of the sixth day in the cave, Hama was carving images on the piece of bone he held. He leaned against the cave wall thinking. "Wing, did you come to save this man? I see that. All these things working together. It cannot be luck. This had to have plan."

"I wondered that, Hama. It makes the spirit man powerful. Power. I don't understand power at all."

Dah looked up. "There is reason for this. I agree with both of you. This is not luck."

Doeoi raised his head. "Too much plan not to be plan. What plan? Not know. But plan. Sure."

"Doeoi, what brought you here?" Wing asked.

Doeoi spoke slowly, sometimes using hand gestures. "My brother and me. We fish in salt water to south. Big wind blow. Our boat made for river. We had gone out of river. Think okay. Not okay. Storm took us. Wind pushed us over the salt water. We in boat long time. We no food. Only water from rain. Hard to find water to drink. With all that water, no water to drink. We sure we die."

"We are glad you alive, Doeoi," Dah said with feeling.

"I grateful man to you."

"Dah," Wing said, "Our boat is partly buried in the sand. How we return in boat?"

"I thought you'd have figured it out," Dah and Hama laughed.

"I no understand," Wing said confused.

"We untie the logs. We roll logs to water. We line up logs. We retie logs. We use boat again."

Wing laughed at how simple it was. "I didn't think!" he said, laughing at himself.

"Good we brought poles inside!" Hama added.

"As soon as I saw that sky," Dah said, "I knew we needed to protect them from blowing away."

"You wise," Doeoi said, making himself part of the conversation.

"He is," Topozelmu said.

"Let's sleep. Tomorrow we return home. It seems Wing has done what he came to do."

"I'll take a short walk first," Topozelmu said.

"I join you?" Wing asked.

"Of course," Topozelmu replied.

They walked along the beach close together. The tide was going out. They left footprints that quickly erased themselves.

Wing reached out and took her hand. Topozelmu was a little surprised, but she didn't object. She released her hand and put her arm around his back. He put his arm around her shoulders. They walked wordlessly for a long distance.

Wing stopped and looked at her. He thought they should turn around. Instead her eyes drew him and he dared before thinking to reach out to kiss her. Instead of recoiling, Topozelmu melted into his kiss and they stood there embracing. One thing led to another and after yet a while longer they started walking back to the cave.

"I loved you first sight, Topozelmu."

"It took me until night with you in my hut. Bort asked me to give you room for a reason."

"He made good decision," Wing said.

"Yes. He did. I'm happy."

"Topozelmu, will you be my wife?"

"Yes. I will be your wife."

"How is it done here?" he asked.

"We return. Bort will announce to all."

"I like that!"

"I do too," she replied and once again they kissed. Then they entered the cave.

The return trip was uneventful. Bort was not in the least surprised about Topozelmu and Wing. He was surprised at the dark-skinned person who returned with them. He liked the stranger. All was well.

Part 3

Five years passed since the rescue of Doeoi. Topozelmu and Wing had three children. When Topozelmu had their first child, Wing was never happier in his life. He also felt a sense of overwhelming responsibility. For a long time he would have to devote his life to see that his young son grew up to be a good man, a contributor to the group, responsible, and loving. He was awed at the process that brought another person into the world. Topozelmu had worked so hard. She'd been in such pain. He knew some husbands took off hunting when their wives went into labor. He refused to leave her side. He caught the slippery little one when he came forth. He fell into Wing's hands as a gift.

When Ahn arrived the labor and delivery went easier for Topozelmu. Wing caught Ahn also and laughed when he realized this one was a girl. He was delighted. By the time Tu came, it wasn't that it was becoming routine, birth was too special for that, but it wasn't as filled with the same degree of surprise for Wing. Tu came into the world screaming and shaking his fists. Wing found that amusing and hoped that wasn't a portent of things to come. Quite the contrary. Once in this world, Tu was calm and a delightfully contented baby.

Doeoi became the husband of Lumi, Dah and Hama's sister. Lumi had fallen in love with Doeoi the moment she saw him. His almost black skin fascinated her and she found his soft tightly curled hair irresistible. They had two children, a boy and girl. Recently Dah, Hama, and their brother, Peza, had gone to other groups where they found wives. Dah and Hama returned with wives, but Peza remained where his wife lived nearer the salt water.

In the five years since he'd left home, Wing had experienced great physical change. Where once he had been a very short young man with a frail looking body, he'd grown into an exceptionally tall man with a body that no longer showed any signs of frailness. Instead his body reflected great strength. Wing had a strong desire to take his family to visit the place where he grew up. He wanted to see his mother and brothers and sister at his former home. He wanted them to meet his family to let them know he lived.

Topozelmu agreed to join the trek. Hama and his wife decided to accompany them. Hama had always wanted to see Popocatépetl closer. They left early one morning carrying great burdens filled with comfort for their journey.

When they reached the pine nut tree, Wing asked them to wait. At the base of the tree he knelt. He took something from his pack and laid it on the ground. From the valley's edge the others couldn't see it. They were not able to hear him say, "Spirit, I touched the feather. You told me not to touch it. I return it and ask for your forgiveness. I have cared for it well. I disobeyed by touching it. I excused myself. I wanted proof that the feather was not a dream. My excuse made no right for disobedience. I return the feather now. I ask for forgiveness."

Wing found quickly that the return trip was very familiar. As they walked he remembered each place he stayed. He knew where the water was. It was a long trek, but the familiarity of it was refreshing. With the feather gone, his pack felt much lighter. He was glad not to be alone. Wing carried an extra heavy load because Topozelmu carried their infant, Tu. Zeb was old enough to walk. Ahn occasionally needed carrying. Elmalla, Hama's wife, was more than willing to help carry when the little girl fatigued. She loved children and was hoping soon to have some of her own.

It wasn't long before they spent the night at the place where Wing had the experience with the bear. Wing could feel the bear's presence again as if it were actually happening. He was relieved it wasn't.

Wing enjoyed being a father. On their evening stops after their last meal of the day, the adults and children would sing the stars out. They sang of past events, of hopes, of joys, of surprises on the trek. They'd make up words on the spot. Some choruses would be used from song to song, some made new. They had a variety of tunes they tended to use and re-use. Ahn loved to sing at night. She'd snuggle close to Wing. She'd sing and suddenly no one heard from Ahn. She drifted to sleep in the middle of her own singing.

Hama would carve animal shapes in pieces of bone. Elmalla would lean against him careful not to pin his arms. She watched him at his carving. She'd never seen anyone make representations of animals. She could tell what each was. Sometimes he lacked good bone and he'd superimpose a carving over another.

As they neared Wing's old homeland, they reached the place where he had stood long ago and looked down on the landscape below. He'd seen the twisted mountains. They still fascinated him. The children were with Dah and Elmalla. He and Topozelmu walked to the edge of the mountaintop to gaze at the scene.

"The earth does seem to have squeezed it all into a tortured shape. Is that damage from earthquakes?"

"I think it must be."

"That's interesting," Topozelmu said.

"What?" Wing asked.

"We've had no earthquake for a long time. We had them almost daily. Now, for a long time—none."

"You're right. Maybe it has come to rest again. I hope it's for a long time."

"Popocatépetl used to smoke a lot. There's nothing there." Topozelmu leaned against him.

Wing drew her away from the edge of the mountain and they headed back to the others. The night was spectacular. Stars were blazing in the sky. With the moon out it was easy to see to walk around in the night.

Wing took the gourd and drank water. He offered it to Topozelmu. She waved it off.

All wrapped in their sleeping skins and slept.

They slept later than usual. They quickly fixed a morning meal. While that was being prepared, Wing took Zeb and Ahn to the edge of the path.

"See that mountain all white at top? Its name?"

"Popocatépetl," Zeb replied.

"I was gonna say that," Ahn complained.

"What's the name of that one?" Wing pointed to the large mountain to the east.

"I don't know," they both replied.

"It's La Malinche," he replied. "You say it. Say it three times. That helps you remember."

They repeated it three times.

"Land low like that. What name?" he asked.

"Valley," Ahn said quickly.

"Good. Both of you answered well today." He headed them back to eat before leaving.

They ate and gathered their things. They began their descent to the valley and the next ascent would

79

be on Popocatépetl. Wing suddenly threw his arms to the side. He was leading so that stopped them all. Each knew when he did that to be absolutely silent. All looked furtively around. Nobody saw anything. Topozelmu thought she heard something clacking. They listened. It was clear Wing was smelling something.

Wing walked very carefully forward. Around a slight curve, he could see what he'd smelled. It was two of the most alarming terror birds he'd ever seen. It caught his breath to realize how much taller they were than he. Wing went to the face of Zeb, his son, and Ahn, his daughter. He signed for them to be quiet. The adults knew something was up. Wing pointed to the glen beyond the forest edge. They'd see it as they passed. He signed: *two terror birds*. They were the biggest terror birds he'd ever seen. Their plumage was stunningly gaudy in color: reds, blues, greens, yellows. He led family and friends past the place. The birds each seemed intent on the other, and they did not detect the people slipping by on the path. Their beaks clattered together as they performed for each other. It was loud. Their feet stamped the earth hard enough for the people to feel it, as far removed as they were.

Ahn was terribly frightened by the terror birds. Elmalla lifted her up and carried her. Ahn buried her face in Elmalla's neck. Elmalla realized quickly that comforting Ahn from fear reduced her own.

By afternoon Wing felt a relief that they'd passed the terror birds. The little group stopped at a massive, widespread oak to rest in the shade. They'd make the next cave by evening, and tomorrow they could reach his old homeland.

The next day they reached the big lake. They spent time there at an overlook, not where animals would come to water.

"I never guessed it was this big," Hama remarked. "It's beautiful."

"I think so. The blue of it like the sky is wonderful in this land." Wing was chewing on a piece of grass.

"I don't suppose it has alligators?" Elmalla asked.

"No," Wing replied. "We're too high in mountains. Too cold for alligators here."

"That's wonderful," she said, wondering whether she might bathe in the lake.

"Wing?" Topozelmu asked having shared Elmalla's thought of the water, "Is there a place to bathe in the lake?"

"There is! Let's go!" He encouraged them to continue on.

They walked around the rim until they came to a coved area where they could tell the lake was shallow.

"This is a good place. Best for children," he said, unloading his burdens.

Wing stripped off his skirt and necklace and ran to the water leaving the others startled as he made great splashes. He came running back and took Zeb by the hand. He ran with Zeb into the water splashing furiously. The others were unburdening themselves quickly preparing to enjoy the water. After the hot trek, this was wonderful. Wing washed sand through his hair and rinsed it. He did the same to Zeb. Then he washed Ahn's hair. He watched Topozelmu come into the water with the baby. He burned for her. She had been the best wife he could dream of having. He adored her. It showed in his smile.

The noise alerted hunters on the other side of the lake. The hunters quickly sought cover to observe the noisy people south of them.

"You ever see them?" Amor asked Zik.

"No."

"They outnumber us."

"Yes," Zik whispered back, "They would be busy protecting their children. We may be about even."

"Let's confront them, then." Amor wanted to have the confrontation over. He had confidence in his and Zik's ability to do this without an elder present. They had risen early to hunt without Itz. Because of it, they enjoyed the day.

Dah was the first to spot the hunters. "People come," he said, in a conversational tone that was anything but conversational.

The people emerged from the water. They put their clothes on. They had the children sit with the women. Wing and Dah stood still awaiting the arrival of the hunters.

When they came closer, Wing laughed heartily and shouted, "Zik! Amor! It's Wing! He ran to them. The hunters stood still as if in disbelief.

Wing didn't look anything like what they remembered except for his smile. The smile was the giveaway. They embraced and wept.

"I thought never to see you again, Brother," Amor said. "You grow so big."

"I thought you dead," Zik said. "You sad hunter. How you survive all this time alone?"

"I wasn't alone all this time. I found people. *Our* people. They come from Puh's son, Bort. Come meet my wife, my children, and friends."

Wing made the introductions. They sat and Topozelmu and Elmalla shared some dried fruit and nuts with the men.

"Oh, Zik, I almost forgot." Wing reached into his pouch he kept on the side of his skirt. "This is yours." He handed Zik the piece of cordage that Zik had used years ago to splint his arm. It was special because Toa, their grandmother made it.

"I had forgotten all about that. Thank you, Wing. All these years you took good care of it."

"I knew it was special to you."

"You are coming home?" Amor asked.

"I want to see you, Zik, Spu, Moot, and our mother. Of course, our grandparents too. I don't care whether I see our father."

"You must know we all thought you dead. Your return to visit will be great shock. Grandmother died. She had bad cough. She buried now. Mother not well. She will be so happy to see you. So will Grandfather. Our father is still just as he was. Moot and Lat have children. Aga moved to another place to be with wife's people. He hated to leave Zik. Zik was good brother. Aga very happy." Amor felt as if he'd talked for a day. He never used so many words. He ate a few more nuts.

"Are you ready to continue? We'll accompany you." Zik said.

"Have you completed a successful hunt yet?" Wing asked in return.

"No. We have some camel left. That will suffice for tonight," Zik assured him.

"Why not let us help finish the hunt and then we go?" Wing suggested.

"You better hunter now?" Zik teased.

"Judge for yourself," Wing replied with a smile.

The women let the children play at the water's edge while the men walked off into the wooded area with spears. This was part of life to them. The little ones had a wonderful time. The baby slept through it.

In very little time the hunters had returned with two deer. The deer were gutted and bled. There was a sense of triumph when Wing asked Zik how he judged his hunting skills.

"You saw that deer and had your spear thrust so fast. I didn't know it was there. Perfect aim. I am in awe, my friend."

"I've had a lot of practice."

"Yes. And no one discouraging you."

"Ah, how true."

"Now, you ready to head home?" Amor asked.

Wing raised an eyebrow at Hama. Hama smiled back.

"We're ready." They gathered their things, put their packs on, and began the trek.

Wing was not planning a long visit. He knew if things turned difficult they'd leave the next day. He hoped it didn't come to that.

Puh was the first to notice.

"Who are these people?" he shouted.

"Your grandson, Wing," Wing shouted back, "with his family and friends."

Puh stood completely still. This huge man claimed to be the short, frail boy who died?

Wing hurried forward and smiled at Puh. Puh recognized the smile. He held his arms out and the two embraced.

"So you're alive," he said.

"Yes, Grandfather. I live. Come meet my wife, children, and friends." Wing introduced them.

Puh accompanied them to the tiny little village. Puh took Wing straight to see Goyah, his mother. She was ill but would be delighted to see Wing. Her hut was so tiny that only Puh and Wing could fit inside with her.

"Goyah?" Puh said. "I bring good news."

"What is it?"

Wing noticed how feeble she had become. It broke his heart.

"You remember Wing?"

"Of course I remember Wing."

"Goyah, he lives. He has come to see you."

Goyah turned and rested on her elbow. She looked at the other person she hadn't noticed.

"Puh, this is giant, not my son." Then she saw Wing smile. "Oh, it is my boy. You alive, my boy. All these years I think you dead. You lived. I so happy to see you. A hug. Now."

Wing crawled over to hold her in his arms. She was nothing but bones, but he loved those bones and handled her with extreme care.

"Mother, I have a wife. I have children. I have friends. I want you to meet them. Are you able?"

"Of course. Tell Moot make me a place outside in shade. Then you carry me out there."

Puh left to find Moot. She had heard the news and was just outside her mother's hut. Quickly she began to make a pallet outside for her mother to use to meet all the people. When it was ready she popped her head into her mother's hut and told her.

"You so big, my boy," she said to Wing, "Take me out there so I meet your people."

Wing lifted her off the bed. She weighed almost nothing. He carried her outside and laid her gently on the pallet. It had been a long time since Goyah had been outside. She breathed in the fresh air. She smiled.

"Mother, this is my wife, Topozelmu. This little one is our newest. His name is Tu."

Topozelmu reached out her hand. Goyah took her hand and held it softly. Goyah smiled. She felt an instant liking for the wife of her son.

"This girl is second child. Ahn."

Goyah smiled at Ahn.

"I happy to meet you, Grandmother," Ahn said. She stooped down and kissed her grandmother's cheek.

Goyah grinned. She reached out and touched the top of Ahn's head.

"This boy is our first born. His name is Zeb." Zeb also kissed his grandmother's cheek.

"This is Hama, a great friend and hunter from my new homeland." Hama took Goyah's hand.

"You good man. You create?"

Hama was clearly startled, his eyes widening, but he only said with great respect, "I carve animal images on bones."

"You create," she said. "I know when I feel your hand. You use different muscles to make lines on bones or rock. Little muscles. These the little ones." She pressed on the little muscles that gave away his effort carving lines on the bones. "Show me."

Hama stooped down and pulled the mammoth bone, still soft, from his bag. "This I do," he said.

Goyah looked off into the sky, eyes unfocused. "This someone find long time ahead. They see your images. They wonder."

Everyone stared at Goyah. Who would have thought she'd know something like that from touching a hand? From looking at a piece of bone. Wing and others wondered. Hama put the bone in his pack. No one doubted her words.

Wing interrupted the moment. "Mother, this is Hama's wife, Elmalla."

"You lovely girl, Elmalla. You have many children. Many children." The old woman looked far into the distance.

Elmalla hoped the old lady was right. She loved children and wanted many.

Itz realized people were gathered near his wife's hut. He'd seen them looking at a bone. He walked over.

"Who these peoples?" he demanded.

Wing stood. He saw that he was two heads taller than his father, if not more. It made him want to laugh, but he stifled the urge.

"It is Wing with family and friends. I am here to visit."

"Wing dead. Who are you?" Itz insisted.

Wing smiled. Suddenly in the far reaches of the man's mind, the smile told him he was in fact looking at his son. The one who ran away.

"You left and lived?" He was incredulous.

"Yes, Father. I left and lived."

"How you live?"

"I hunted for my food. After a long time I found the people of Bort, your brother. I live in Bort's village."

"Bort," his father snorted. "Bort good hunter."

"I agree," he said.

"You poor hunter."

"That's not true," Zik said. "Before any of us saw that huge deer over there, Wing had his spear flying and his aim was perfect."

"Humph," Itz said. He walked over to look at the deer.

"You still lousy hunter!" he muttered.

Wing walked purposely over to his father. Goyah watched with concern. Wing grabbed the man, pinning his arms to his sides and lifting him off the ground. "You listen! You understand! I come to visit my people. I love them. I did not come to listen to your discouraging words. You will keep your discouraging words trapped in your mouth. You speak discouraging words now? I tie you up on a tree until I ready to go home. You understand?" He put Itz back down.

Itz was overwhelmed at Wing's strength. He felt foolish dangling there with a son talking to him like that, but he did not dare speak. He feared his son would tie him on a tree. He did not know this Wing, this giant of a man with incredible strength. He didn't want to fear his son, but he did. He lowered his head in silence.

Wing looked at the man. He realized his father feared him. It was a revelation.

"For all the past discouraging words, Father, I forgive you."

"I don't need your forgiveness," Itz said firmly with defiance.

"Ah, but Father, I have no concern about your need. It is my need. I need to forgive you. I lay down all the ill will. I've carried it all these years. I turn loose of it in forgiving you. It will be part of my life no more forever. I am free of it. Freed! Freedom! I have freedom from your discouragement forever."

Itz looked at him in utter disbelief. The old man failed to understand. What he understood is that he feared this child. He had no idea what he might do next. And he was huge.

Wing glanced at his mother. She was shedding tears with a smile on her face. Wing understood. His mother understood the words of forgiveness.

Wing had not discussed with Topozelmu what he did. It had simply come to him. He felt somehow connected to the wrinkled spirit man from the golden mist. He had forgiven his father. He had been forgiven for the feather disobedience. No longer did he fear a lightning strike.

Topozelmu felt that Wing had said something profound. She put the words in memory. It was something to remember for a lifetime. Never fail to forgive. That way you were freed.

The people began to prepare the largest of the deer for their night meal. They quartered the smaller one, carried it to the little pond nearby, and submerged the pieces holding them underwater with rock weights.

Itz walked off to the forest edge. He sat on a rock looking over the slope of Popocatépetl. He wanted to strike back at this son who had returned from the dead. He would do it, but the man Wing had become frightened him. He knew the man would make him a laughing point of the village if he crossed him. Itz decided it was in his best interest to stay clear of Wing. He didn't want to say any discouraging words. It would be best if he kept a great distance.

Wing returned to Goyah.

She beamed a smile that surprised him. "You have gained wisdom my son," she said very quietly. "You know the spirit?"

Wing flinched at the word, spirit. He nodded.

"It is a good thing. You fear?"

"Perhaps a little. I don't encounter him often enough for him to be familiar."

"I understand."

"You do?" Wing was amazed, yet when he thought about it, of all the living people in his old homeland, she'd be the one he'd suspect would know spirit things.

"Of course. That's how I know."

"Does he appear out of a golden mist as a very wrinkled old man?"

"I know of what you speak. Trust this spirit, Wing. Don't cross him."

"I trust, Mother. Don't fear for me. I won't cross him. Bort's son crossed the spirit and was killed by a lightning strike. I did cross the spirit. I made it right. I have been forgiven."

His mother shuddered.

"How long you stay, my son?"

"Considering my effect on Father, I think we return tomorrow. I just wanted to see you. I wanted to say words to you. I love you. I always loved you."

"I know, Son. I always loved you. I love your family and friends. You made good choice to leave."

"I can go home now. I know we have love in hearts. And I can live completely freed from early abuse."

"Wing, that pleases me. It makes me freed to die. I die soon. I am past ready. You freed my last hold on this world. I wanted to know what became of you. I thought you lived. And, you did. You live well. Very well."

The call to the meal came as the sun set. All were hungry and that hunger was well rewarded with good meat and a wide variety of vegetables and fruits. Wing met with Hama and they decided to leave after the morning meal. A little jolt rocked the earth.

"We talked about no earthquakes earlier. Have we called this one," Topozelmu laughed and others joined her.

After everyone was asleep Itz still wandered around. He looked at his son. He glanced at a small boulder, considering crushing Wing's head with it. He reasoned it would make noise and he would be killed. Then, he remembered the bone. He found the pack resting against a tree. There was more than one bone. Itz removed the bones and estimated their weight. He wrapped the rock equivalents to the bones in the leather that had covered the bones. He placed the substitute back into the pack just as he'd found the bones. He looked at Wing sleeping. He sneered. Itz took the bones a short distance away and buried them. Then he lay down to sleep.

No one paid the small quake any mind. It was expected in this land. The people soon forgot it had happened.

The next morning, they ate and were on their way. Amor and Zik accompanied them to the big lake and from there they went their separate ways. They trekked well into the early evening when they stopped at one of their caves for the night.

Several small earthquakes made the land quiver. There was jesting that if they'd still been trekking they wouldn't have noticed the quiver.

As the days passed, the small group noticed numbers of small earthquakes. Because it was such a common occurrence, they paid it little heed. Ungulates on the other hand were not lying still chewing their cud but rather walking aimlessly around the valley, looking for something which they could not seem to find. They seemed disturbed. Ahn noticed but said nothing.

What was given some attention is that Hama had lost his carved bones. He was undone. He couldn't imagine how he lost them. He'd taken great care to keep them safe. The image he carved of the gomphothere was incomplete. He had planned more work on it. What he and none of them ever guessed is that Itz had seen him work on it. To spite them, he'd taken the bones and hidden them.

When they reached the pine nut tree there was a huge earthquake. It literally caused the people to fall to the ground. The earth in their lifetimes had not jarred that strongly.

"Let's climb the hill quickly. I want to see!" Hama shouted.

They struggled under the weight of their burdens, children, and concern to reach the top of the hill at the V that led to their homeland. At the top they could see Popocatépetl. It was fine. To the east, however, there was a huge plume of dark black and gray smoke billowing upwards. High. So high they were speechless. They'd never seen such a thing. Huge sounds of explosions reached their ears. They hurried to their home. They wanted all to be together in this time of abnormality.

None of them had seen a volcano erupt. They were unsure what they witnessed. The next day while the volcano spewed out more ejecta, Hama, Dah, and Wing took their spears and little food and traveled fast. They climbed the tallest peak they could find. From there they could see the eruption of La Malinche. A huge lump formed in Wing's throat. His voice caught. He understood that all the people he'd just visited were dead. They were buried in the ash falling from the material La Malinche spit out. They returned to report what they'd found to the others.

Months later, the eruption cloud had passed away. At a gathering Wing said, "I would like very much to make fast travel. I want to be sure my family perished. I want to know."

Dah said, "I will go with you."

Both wives encouraged them to make the quick trip. The men left the next morning.

They set off before the morning meal. They traveled very fast, often jogging. Both were in excellent condition for such a quick trip. They traveled far earlier and later than most trekkers.

"Could they have survived?" Dah asked.

"It depends on how deep the falling substance was. It had to affect their breathing. It could have buried them completely. My mother was ready to die. Not one of rest was ready to die. They'd have fought to live."

A great shaking of the ground occurred and mammoths trumpeted in an unusual manner. The two men stood up from their sleeping skins to see what was happening. They saw a herd of mammoths running fast down the valley as if frightened. They looked about to see what had frightened the animals. They had no evidence. They could occasionally feel little shudders in the earth, but not enough to be considered frightening. The men shrugged it off and went to sleep.

The next day they arose and ate some jerky. They began their trek to the first hill from which they could have a good view of the two big mountains and into the valley. Both were dumbstruck. La Malinche had blown its head off. The area was an ugly mess of a gaping wound and black, gray, and tan material littering the ground. Popocatépetl's lovely white top was stained. This was devastating.

"Do you think we've seen enough?" Dah asked.

"Not sure."

"You worry. Think some may be alive? Maybe escaped?"

"It could be possible."

"Then, come on. Let's go." Dah led the way. It was clear that Wing was brokenhearted to see what he saw. How anyone might have survived the devastation was beyond Dah's reasoning, but he considered Wing. If he were Wing, he might want to be sure.

The two jogged through the area, ash lay in various layers as they traveled. It was slightly caustic to the skin, they discovered. They didn't know whether it was because it was sharp or whether something in the ash itself bothered their skin. They had a fright on the third day of traversing the ashfall zone. La Malinche spewed forth a short lived plume. It was enough to serve as a warning. Wing assured Dah if he wanted to turn back, that would be understandable. As for himself, he'd continue. Dah would not desert his friend. The two continued.

Wing had to depend on land shapes, since nothing else remained. They finally reached the area where he expected his family's village should be. The area was covered in ash. Wing fell to his knees and wept. He had hoped to find someone. After he gathered himself together, he thought he heard something.

He listened carefully, looked around, and didn't see anything. Finally movement caught his eye. There beyond him was a pathetic little creature. He and Dah studied it for quite some time before they realized it was a baby raccoon. Wing picked up the whimpering little creature. Most of its coat had been singed off. Its feet were burned on the bottom. It was so tiny. He wondered whether it was weaned.

Dah watched Wing. He thought surely his friend had sense enough to leave the animal where he found it, but he guessed wrong. He watched silently as Wing tucked the baby raccoon into his bag. The two turned wordlessly and began to retrace their steps.

Dah and Wing stopped for the night. They might have kept going a little longer, but it was just too dark. Dah was shocked to see Wing let the raccoon sip water from his gourd. He also found it unbelievable that Wing gave the little animal a chewed piece of his jerky. The pathetic little animal seemed truly grateful.

"What will you do with it at home?" Dah asked.

"I will help it heal. Then, it can go to find others. It visit for a while."

"What if the children cling to it?" he asked having a sense of how children would feel about it.

"I will tell them. They know raccoon is animal. It will need other raccoons. It free to come and go. We enjoy while here. We no trap it."

"I see." He hoped Wing would be successful.

"Wing?" Dah said one evening as they ate duck from a small pond they passed.

"Yes?" Wing replied with a groan, his belly overfull.

"You came here. I'm glad. You make life interesting. We found Doeoi because of you. We see mountain belch up much ash because of you. You make our life better."

"I grateful for those words, Dah. I grateful for Bort's people. All Bort's people good to live with. You excellent friend. You excellent hunter. I enjoy trip with you."

As they arrived home, the people came out to meet them. Topozelmu raced to him. He threw his arms around her and wept.

"They all gone?" she asked.

"They all gone," he replied. "Thank you."

"Why you thank me?"

"You urged us to go. To go when we did. I was willing to put off visit a little longer. To put off would have missed them."

"It worked out well, Wing. What's that?"

She jumped when she saw the burned animal crawl from the pouch.

"At my village I look for people. Nothing. All dead. Then I hear tiny voice. It raccoon—burnt, hair off, lost. I couldn't leave to die out there."

"I'm glad. I'll help it heal."

"I hoped. Thank you, Wife."

They headed to their hut. Most of the people hadn't seen the raccoon. Wing placed his spears carefully in the corner of the hut, tying them back to avoid breakage now that the hut held five people.

"Let me see the little guy," Topozelmu said. The children came in and saw the raccoon.

"What is it?" Zeb asked.

"Raccoon. It was burnt in the ash. We let it visit here. It need to heal. Then can go to its people."

"Ohhhh," Ahn said. "Can I hold it?"

"Not now. It burnt. In pain," Wing said gently. "It will come to you maybe. Depend on its want. You don't force it. Understand me."

"I understand, Father." Ahn wanted to hold the raccoon, to cuddle it, but she fully understood her father and was obedient.

In time as the raccoon healed, it chose to attach itself to Eku. It followed Eku wherever she went. It would pat her face and play with her hair. It would run with her where she ran. It would bring her bits of food.

That rankled Ahn, who felt a proprietary interest in the raccoon. She became jealous of Eku. Wing had to step in. He took Ahn for a long walk where they discussed the sense of freedom, because he wanted her to know that the raccoon was free to decide what to do. He wanted her to understand how it would be to be captured and have to do what another wanted her to do, not what she wanted to do. He remained on their walk until he was certain she understood. He wanted Ahn to learn that having another do what you wanted, when they didn't want to, was fake. Trying to capture the raccoon would make it turn on her, because she would be hurting it, depriving it of its freedom. It would be waiting for any opportunity to escape. It would never be a happy captive. He was also unwilling for her to be eaten by jealousy. He wanted her to develop her enjoyment of freedom and to give that freedom to others willingly, as part of her healthy being. That was, he knew, the way to live.

"I had bad thoughts," she finally said to him.

"You are young, Ahn. We all learn to throw away our worst ways and hold tight to the good ones. I want you to be good woman like your mother. We all have to learn. That's what being young for. Learn. Learn well. Live right when grown."

"I'm glad you my father," she said and hugged him.

"I'm glad you my daughter," he told her.

He looked through the tree tops to the sky. I'm so glad I forgave my father, he thought. So glad he knew it. It is hard to be a good father. Require much thinking and love. I was right to forgive my father. Yes, right.

He and Ahn held hands and walked back to the village singing their favorite songs on the way.

The little village that Bort started had eleven people when Wing arrived. It grew to the size of twenty-five and then would grow even larger. It was a good place to live. During the lifetime of Wing and his children, there were no more explosive volcanic events. Wing lived to be a very old and wrinkled man. People considered him not only an elder but also a leader. Topozelmu also lived a very long life and she, too, became a wrinkled old one. After she died, Wing lived six months and died in his sleep one night, convinced that he would go to the spirit place to be reunited with Topozelmu.

Bibliography

Christopher Hardaker, *The First American,* Career Press, 2007.

"Art of Americas from 30,000 BC," *LIFE Magazine*, Vol 49, No. 7, page 86, August 15, 1960.

Laland, Kevin, et al., "does evolutionary theory need a rethink?" Nature, Vol 514, Issue 7521. Comment. 8 October 2014.

Sample, Ian, "Skull of Homo Erectus throws story of human evolution into disarray." www.theguardian.com/science/2013/oct/17/skull-homo-erectus-human-evolution

http://pleistocenecoalition.com/ (See "Pleistocene Coalition News")

http://patagoniamonsters.blogspot.com/2011/01/ostrander-skull-supposedly-erectus.html

https://www.academia.edu/3094479/The_Forgotten_
Collector_Josef_Anton_Dorenberg_1846-1935_ (Click
on "Get the PDF")

http://pleistocenecoalition.com/vanlandingham/
VanLandingham_2006.pdf

http://news.nationalgeographic.com/
news/2010/02/100217-crete-primitive-humans-mariners-
seafarers-mediterranean-sea/

https://grahamhancock.com/hardakerc1/

http://archaeologica.boardbot.com/viewtopic.php?p=23279

http://newgeology.us/presentation32.html

http://www.dailymail.co.uk/sciencetech/article-1212060/
Ancient-skeletons-discovered-Georgia-threaten-overturn-
theory-human-evolution.html

There is a larger bibliography at my website:
http://www.booksbybonnye.com

Google Valsequillo, Hueyatlaco, Juan Armena Comacho,
Pleistocene Coalition, Virginia Steen McIntyre

Google images for Valsequillo archaeological site

Google Valsequillo hoax for the opposition

CPSIA information can be obtained
at www.ICGtesting.com
Printed in the USA
LVHW080409291222
736127LV00014B/1175